Coulson Kernahan

Sorrow and Song

Coulson Kernahan

Sorrow and Song

ISBN/EAN: 9783744769075

Printed in Europe, USA, Canada, Australia, Japan

Cover: Foto ©Andreas Hilbeck / pixelio.de

More available books at **www.hansebooks.com**

SORROW AND SONG.

BY

COULSON KERNAHAN,

AUTHOR OF

"A BOOK OF STRANGE SINS," "A DEAD MAN'S DIARY," ETC.

LONDON:

WARD, LOCK & BOWDEN, LIMITED,

WARWICK HOUSE, SALISBURY SQUARE, E.C.

NEW ORK AND MELBOURNE.

1894.

TO THEODORE WATTS,

POET AND CRITIC,

THESE PAGES ARE WITH ADMIRATION, AFFECTION, AND GRATITUDE INSCRIBED.

"My experience of men of letters is, that for kindness of heart they have no equal. I contrast their behaviour to the young and struggling with the harshness of the Lawyer, the hardness of the Man of Business, the contempt of the Man of the World, and am proud to belong to their calling."—MR. JAMES PAYN'S *Literary Recollections*.

PREFACE.

In two of these papers—those on Heine and Robertson—I have attempted a study of some aspects of personality from real life, just as in *A Book of Strange Sins* I endeavoured to bring out certain sides of human nature by depicting characters drawn entirely from imagination. The other articles, though not altogether impersonal, are more critical in intention. As with the exception of Robertson of Brighton all with whom I deal are poets, and all are notable for the sadness of their life or of their song, my title needs no explanation. The papers have been entirely re-cast and re-written since their appearance in the *Fortnightly Review*, the *London Quarterly Review*, the *New York Independent*, Mr. A. H. Miles's *Poets and Poetry of the Century*, etc., to the editors of which I am indebted for permission to print them here.

C. K.

CONTENTS.

A PROBLEM IN PERSONALITY.

B

"THE Spirit of the world,
Beholding the absurdity of men—
Their vaunts, their feats—let a sardonic smile
For one short moment wander o'er his lips:
That smile was Heine!"

MATTHEW ARNOLD.

A PROBLEM IN PERSONALITY.

I.

OVER Goethe's grave rests a serene after-glow like that which follows the tranquil setting of a sun : the spot where Heine lies is lit only by the wild trailing of light which marks the track of a fallen star. Goethe sat afar off upon his intellectual throne, supremely, almost sublimely self-centred and self-confident. He husbanded his genius as a merchant husbands his money; and, like the merchant, invested it always to the best advantage. He never spent himself or his powers to no purpose, and he lived to be more than eighty. Heine, on the other hand, was a prodigal and a spendthrift, who drew upon his capital, and he died at the comparatively early age of fifty-six. Goethe's voice is the voice of an infinitely wise man; but the haunting songs of Heine strike an intimate note in the heart, and stir us as strangely as when we hear again some unremembered snatch of song to which we have listened in our childhood.

He is a magician, an enchanter. His pen is sometimes a painter's brush, with which he dashes off, in a few bold strokes, a picture which calls to us, as it were, from the canvas; at others it is a conductor's baton, and directs a choir of invisible musicians. He was the wittiest and the wickedest of Germans, if, indeed, he was not the first to prove the adaptability of the German language for wit. Humourists and satirists had not been wanting, but their gambols were somewhat elephantine; and the brilliant sword-play and sallies of Heine bewildered and perplexed his less agile countrymen. He discusses the Religion and Philosophy of Germany—subjects upon which few Germans could be anything but " solid"; and though he writes learnedly, his touch is so light that there is not a dull line in the book. Even his comments on the trivial side-issues of the party questions of the hour (and of all stale and fly-blown things, is anything staler than the

petty personalities of bygone petty politics ?)
may be read with entertainment to-day.
As a politician Heine was too capricious
and untrustworthy to win the confidence
of any party, for he was regarded, and
not unjustly, with suspicion by each. His
nature was lacking in the element which
gives tenacity of purpose. He was of every
opinion and faithful to none—an imperialist
who would have all men equal, a democrat
who loathed the democracy. As a matter
of fact, his insight was too keen to allow
him to become—what an enthusiast generally is—a man of one idea. Theoretically
Heine was a republican; but not all the
drum-beating, flag-waving, and frenzied cries
of "Liberty, Equality, and Fraternity" in
which the communists indulged could con-

ceal from him the fact that these very men who made such boast of their liberty were but the tools and slaves of two or three unscrupulous schemers, ten times more tyrannical than the unfortunate monarch of whom they had disposed. On the other hand, although there was no more ardent admirer of power, as incarnate in Napoleon, than Heine, he was too far-seeing to overlook the gigantic blots which disfigured the Napoleonic system of government; and consequently he turned from imperialism with the same dissatisfaction with which he had turned from republicanism. He saw both sides of the question, and, recognizing faults on each, could not make up his mind which to espouse. Hence he passed his life in a state of chronic half-heartedness, drifting this way or that according to the promptings of self-interest or of his own undisciplined impulses.

His religion was as elastic as his politics, and presented as many contradictions. He was by turns an atheist and a theist, a pantheist and a deist, a pagan and a Jew. At heart Heine was by no means irreligious; but just as he loved—sentimentalist though he sometimes was — to masquerade as a cynic, so he tried to conceal the sincerity of his religious feelings by writing what was audaciously profane. There are men, it need scarcely be said, almost incapable of religious ecstasy or uplifting thought, whose actions are above reproach; just as there are men who feel deeply, pray earnestly, and sing hymns with eyes overflowing with heartfelt tears, whose lives will not bear too close an examination. It is with the latter class that the German Aristophanes must be numbered; and although by no stretch of imagination can we picture Heine hymn-singing, shedding repentant tears, or maintaining, even on his death-bed, other semblance than that of the sceptic and the cynic, the sincerity of his religious feeling seems certain, and his blasphemy must be regarded as mere display. In his writings, as in his life, Heine habitually followed inclination rather than conscience. Let a brilliant thought occur to him, and—no matter how unjust or profane it might be —he wrote it down, and made it public, choosing deliberately to circulate what he knew to be slanderous, rather than forego the pleasure of saying something smart. The coarseness which so often disfigures his work was attributable to the same abandonment of every social and moral obligation. With his usual shrewdness, Heine was not slow to realize that indelicate allusions—if for no other reason than that they were by common consent avoided—afforded ready opportunity for cheaply acquiring the reputation of being an original wit; and of such opportunity he was quite unscrupulous enough to avail himself. He would slander his nearest and dearest friend, if in so doing he could display his own abilities to shining advantage; and he would make capital out of subjects that he should have counted sacred, and "copy" out of the holiest feelings of his heart. At one

time we find him writing of the Bible, the
" Memoirs of God," as he called it, in a
strain which shows that, in spite of his
scepticism, there still survived in Heine's
nature something of that almost sublime
fidelity to the faith of his fathers, and
reverence for its sacred books, which a
Jew is said never, in his heart of heart, to
lose. "What a book!" he says in his
monograph on Börne. "Vast and wide as
the world, rooted in the abysses of creation,
and towering up beyond the blue secrets of
heaven. Sunrise and sunset, promise and
fulfilment, birth and death, the whole drama
of humanity, are all in this book."

At another time he makes its traditions
the butt of his too ready wit. And though
the Hebrew blood in Heine never allowed

him in his secret soul to dispossess himself of his faith in the God of his forefathers, he bowed the knee by turns to Jehovah and to Jove ; and when his unbelieving moods were on him, he treated the one with as scant reverence as the other. Has anything more audacious been put into words than his description of the death of deism ?—

"A peculiar awe, a mysterious piety, forbids our writing more to-day. Our heart is full of shuddering compassion ; it is the old Jehovah himself who is preparing for death. We have known him so well from his cradle in Egypt, where he was reared among the divine calves and crocodiles, the sacred onions, ibises, and cats. We have seen him bid farewell to these companions of his childhood, and to the obelisks and sphinxes of his native Nile, to become in Palestine a little god-king amidst a poor shepherd people, and to inhabit a temple-palace of his own. We have seen him later coming into contact with the Assyrian-Babylonian civilization, renouncing his all-too-human passions, no longer giving vent to fierce wrath and vengeance, at least no longer thundering at every trifle. We have seen him migrate to Rome, the capital, where he abjures all national prejudice, and proclaims the celestial equality of all nations, and with such fine phrases establishes an opposition to the old Jupiter, and intrigues ceaselessly till he obtains supreme authority, and from the Capitol rules the city and the world, *urbem et orbem.* We have seen how, growing still more spiritualized, he becomes a loving father, a universal friend of man, a benefactor of the world, a philanthropist; but all this could avail him nothing!

"Hear ye not the bells resounding? Kneel down. They are bringing the sacrament to a dying god!"

This passage is peculiarly Heinesque in its audacity; and Heinesque and individual his work—whether in prose or verse—always is. In some of his songs a stanza, a couplet, or even a line, is sufficient to bespeak its author. This may be said with equal truth of other singers, but not seldom it is the result of their limited range. They strike always a certain keynote, which, from repetition, becomes familiar. Or it may be that they run their molten thought so often into one mould that it sets at last into an easily recognizable mannerism. The reverse is the case with Heine. He often repeats an idea, but rarely the same form of expression. He sweeps the poetic gamut in a single song. He can vary with every verse the emotions he calls into play. Some of his characteristic lyrics open with the wailing of a broken heart. The lines seem to drip blood as we read them. Then there flashes across the page, with the suddenness of purple lightning, one of those deadly dagger-stabs with which Heine struck at many a reputation; and then there is a sudden change in the music, and the verses skip and leap, ripple and run, as if to the accompaniment of dancing feet. In the next stanza, it may be, he holds us hushed and spell-bound, as when we stand at sundown in the darkening aisles of an ancient minster ; and then he startles the silence, which himself has created, with a wild burst of mocking and ribald laughter. So is it with all he writes. He is a creature of the moment, tossed hither and thither by his moods and passions, as withered leaves are whirled by autumn winds. He is by turns a moralist and a libertine, a Frenchman and a German, a Greek and a Jew. In his wildest gaiety there is a glitter of tear-drops, in his loudest laughter the catch of a sob. In some of his love songs, a verse which is as sweet as sea-breezes wafted across fields of blossoming clover, is followed by one in which we feel the hot breath of the sensualist upon our cheek. But it is with the voluptuaries, rather than with the sensualists, that Heine must be classed, and a voluptuary he remained to the end.

"In all ages," he says, "there are to be found men in whom the capacity of enjoyment is incomplete ; men with stunted senses and compunctious frames, for whom all the grapes in the garden of God are sour, who see in every Paradise-apple the enticing serpent, and who seek in self-abnegation their triumph, and in suffering their sole joy. On the other hand, we find in all ages men of robust growth, natures filled with the pride of life, who fain carry their heads right haughtily ; all the stars and the roses greet them with sympathetic smile ; they listen delightedly to the melodies of the nightingale and Rossini ;

C

they are enamoured of good fortune, and of the flesh of Titian's pictures; to their hypocritical companions to whom such things are a torment, they answer in the words of Shakespeare's character, ' Dost thou think because thou art virtuous, there shall be no more cakes and ale ? ' "

Thus Heine wrote in the full flush of health and manhood. In after life, when health and manhood were gone, he spoke often and bitterly of " God's satire weighing heavily upon him." " The Great Author of the Universe, the Aristophanes of heaven," he says, " was bent on demonstrating with crushing force to me, the little earthly German Aristophanes, how my wittiest sarcasms are only pitiful attempts at jesting in comparison with His, and how miserably

I am beneath Him in humour, in colossal mockery."

This is a wild utterance and bitter; but, to realize its exceeding bitterness, one should compare such passages as Heine's panegyric on Italian women—" I love those pale, elegiac countenances from which great black eyes shed forth their love-pain. I love the dark tints of those proud necks : their first love was Phœbus, who kissed them brown. I love even that over-ripe bust with its purple points, as if amorous birds had been pecking at it. But, above all, I love that genial gait, that dumb music of the body, those limbs that move in sweetest rhythm, voluptuous, pliant, with divine enticement" —with the cries of agony which rose from the " mattress-grave," where for eight long years Heine lay in the tortures of a living death. "I have to be carried like a child. The most horrible convulsions. My right hand begins to die." "I have endured more sorrows than the Spanish Inquisition ever invented!" "Ah! why must a human creature suffer so much!"

His malady was a softening of the spinal marrow, and his sufferings were awful. His back became bent and twisted, his body wasted away, as did his legs, which at last became soft and without feeling — "like cotton," as he expressed it.

"He lay on a pile of mattresses," wrote a lady, who visited Heine during his illness, "his body wasted so that it seemed no bigger than a child's under the sheet which covered him, the eyes closed, and the face altogether like the most painful and wasted *Ecce Homo* ever painted by some old German painter."[1] "Of a truth I was terrified; my heart contracted when I saw Heine," says Alfred Meissner, who visited the dying poet in 1849, "and when he stretched out to me his shrunken hand . . . This hand was nearly transparent, and of a pallor and softness of which I have perhaps never seen the like. . . . He told me of his almost uninterrupted torments, of his helplessness. . . . He depicted to me how he himself had become nearly like a ghost, how he looked down upon his poor, broken, racked body like a spirit already departed, and living in a sort of interregnum. He described

[1] Lord Houghton's *Last Days of Heinrich Heine.*

his nights and their tortures, when the
thought of suicide crept nearer and nearer
to him, . . . and truly horrible was it
when he, at last, in fearful earnest and
in suppressed voice, cried out, ' Think on
Günther, Bürger, Kleist, Holderlin, Grabbe,
and the wretched Lenau : some curse lies
heavy on the poets of Germany !' "

Although he became totally blind of one
eye, and the disease so affected the other
that the lid would not remain up, but had
to be raised with his finger before he could
see, Heine did not discontinue writing ; and,
indeed, no inconsiderable portion of his work
was produced at this time. The picture
drawn by his biographer, Mr. Stigand—in
which Heine is described as sitting, propped
up with pillows, on his " mattress-grave,"

lifting with one hand the lid of his paralyzed eye, and with the other tracing painfully large letters upon a sheet of paper—is one of the most pathetic in all literature, and none the less so for the fact that Heine himself often made light of his martyrdoms. His wild wit and humour never deserted him, and his sufferings were often the subject of his ghastly jests. He told the doctor that if his nerves were on show at the Paris Exhibition they would, beyond question, take a gold medal as being unsurpassed in their susceptibility to torture. "He took to reading medical treatises, or rather to having them read to him, on the nature of his disease," writes Mr. Stigand, "and he remarked that his studies would be of use to him by and by, for he would give lectures in heaven, and convince his hearers how badly physicians on earth understood the treatment of softening of the spinal marrow."[1] Another time he said that the worms would soon have his body, but that he did not grudge them their banquet, and was only sorry he could offer them nothing but bones. "But do I still exist?" he wrote in his preface to the *Romancero;* "my body is so shrivelled up that barely anything remains of me but my voice. . . . My measure has long ago been taken for my coffin, also for my necrology; but I die so slowly that the process is as tiresome for myself as for my friends. Yet patience! everything has an end. You will some

---

[1] *The Life, Work, and Opinions of Heinrich Heine.* By William Stigand.

morning find the show shut up where the puppet play of my humour pleased you so often."

It was on February 17, 1856, that this end came. When told that death was approaching, Heine received the news calmly, and in reply to a question whether he had made his peace with heaven, he replied, "*Dieu me pardonnera : c'est son métier.*"

He died at four o'clock in the morning and his face as seen in death is said to have borne a striking resemblance—not only in its dignity and beauty, but in the contour of the features—to the face of Christ.

———————

II.

In the lives of most men—especially of men of high intellectual distinction—there comes, consciously or unconsciously, a time when they stand, as it were, at the parting of two roads, and are called upon to make choice for themselves in regard to some question of supreme moment. And it not seldom happens, that as is their choice at this crisis of their career, so for the most part is the aim and drift of their after life. In attempting to follow out for ourselves one or more of the many tendencies which play an important part in any single soul, it is very necessary that the man's mental attitude and his surroundings at the time of this crisis, as well as the circumstances which determined his previous career, be taken into consideration; and in the case of Heine these circumstances are of unusual moment. Of that ill-fated attachment to his cousin Amalie, which was the inspiration of many of his most passionate songs, we shall probably never know the absolute truth. That his suit was received with apparent encouragement at first, but was ultimately unconditionally rejected, every reader of his story is aware; and it is certain that this rejection plunged him, for the time at least, into profound gloom and despair, and did much to embitter his nature at the outset of his life. But this disappointment has been put forward too often as an excuse for his many excesses;

to this one cause too much of his savage moroseness and cynicism has been attributed; for there were other circumstances which played an even more important part in making Heine what he was.

"In my cradle," he once said, "lay my line of life, marked out from beginning to end." To be born a Jew in Germany towards the end of the last century was little less than a calamity. "The Jews throughout Germany," says Mr. Stigand, "were treated up to the time of the entry of the French as a race of pariahs. The law took as little account of them as of wolves and foxes. Against murder, robbery, violence, and insult they had no redress. Massacres of Jews took place at various towns in Germany late in the century. At Eastertide and other festivals the populace regarded it as their sport and their right to hunt the Jews through the streets, to break their windows with stones, and to sack their houses. In most towns they were forced to live separate from the rest of the inhabitants in their own quarter, into which they were shut with gates every night, and on Sundays they were obliged to wear a peculiar dress. No Jew dared appear on a public promenade without danger of stoning. At Frankfort twenty-five Jews only were allowed to marry in the year, in order that the accursed race might not increase too rapidly. From this abominable state of persecution . . . the Jewish population of Germany were freed at once by the entrance of the French troops: but their emancipation only lasted as long as the French rule. After the liberation of Germany and the final defeat of the French troops, they were thrust back again, in spite of royal pledges to the contrary, into the old pariah condition, only to be finally released from it by the Revolution of 1848." [Eight years before Heine's death.]

To this wicked and relentless persecution much of Heine's Ishmaelitish moroseness of spirit was due. He was an Ishmaelite, indeed, who cherished a sense of injustice and injury,—not merely against his fellow-men, but against his Maker. It seemed, he profanely said, as if the Deity, Who was once "the God of Abraham, Isaac, and Jacob, and was called Jehovah, but was now become so moral, so cosmopolitan, and universal, would like not to remember any more that He was of Palestinian origin, and nourished a secret grudge against the poor Jews who knew Him in His first rough estate, and now put Him in mind daily, in their synagogues, of his former obscure national relations."

As a consequence of this persecution of the Jews, no occupation except that of a school-master or a trader was, in Heine's time, open to one of the despised nationality. To him, however, it was represented that if he would renounce the Jewish faith, and by being baptized make outward profession of Christianity, a civil appointment would be placed at his disposal; and, acting partly upon the advice of so-called friends, but chiefly upon the promptings of his own sordid and self-seeking nature, he gave his consent to a proposal which should never have received his serious consideration.

It is much to be regretted that at this supreme crisis in Heine's life, his belief in God, in man, and in womanhood had fallen away from him. Had he been a man of principle and of character—such a man, for instance, as his English contemporary Frederick Robertson, who, when he lost faith in all that he had once held most sacred, still clung with desperate tenacity (like a shipwrecked mariner to a spar) to the one belief that, though all else might fail him, it yet "must be right to do right"—Heine would not thus have sold his soul, as Esau sold his birthright, for a mess of pottage. But of such saving grace as that displayed by Robertson, Heine was not possessed, and so it came about that—unsupported as he was by any sense of principle, unsustained by any religious belief — it seemed to him, at the moment, but a small matter whether he wore the outward badge of the Jew or the Christian.

How bitterly he repented his apostasy is known to all; and his sense of self-abasement was intensified by the fact that the promised appointment for which he had sold himself was never given to him. " I often get up in the night," he said, when writing to a friend on the subject of his baptism, —" I often get up in the night, and stand before the glass, and curse myself!"

But no curses could restore to him his lost self-respect, and from this point Heine

D

seems to have gone steadily down-hill. Re-
viled as a traitor by the Jews and distrusted
by the Christians ; embittered and made
reckless by his unhappy love affair ; con-
sumed with fierce self-loathing, and cherish-
ing wild resentment against God and man
for the persecution to which all of his race
were subjected,—is it altogether to be won-
dered at that a man like Heine, moody and
sensitive to morbidness, should thenceforth
have abandoned himself, in defiance and
despair, to the promptings of his undisciplined nature and the gratification of his
unhallowed desires ?

III.

In *The Guardian Angel*—professedly a novel, but in reality a psychological study —Dr. Oliver Wendell Holmes quotes a singular saying, for which he gives no authority : — " This body, in which we journey across the isthmus between the two oceans, is not a private carriage, but an omnibus." From this strange text Dr. Holmes preaches an equally strange sermon, in the course of which he says that " it is by no means certain that our individual personality is the single inhabitant of these our corporeal frames "; and he then goes on to tell us that "there is an experience recorded which, so far as it is received in evidence, tends to show that some who have long been dead may enjoy a kind of secondary and imperfect yet self-conscious life in the bodily tenements which we are in the habit of considering exclusively our own." How many strange and conflicting personalities met in the single person of Heinrich Heine we shall never know; and until the comparatively neglected science of heredity be given the place which its importance demands, our psychology, like much of our pathology, must remain mere guesswork.

Sooner or later heredity will have to be studied more widely and more assiduously than many, if not most, of the infinitely less interesting and infinitely less momentous sciences which now occupy the attention of scientific men.

It will have its professors and its colleges as surely as there is a College of Surgeons to-day; and no physician will attempt to diagnose a complex or difficult case without consultation with a professional hereditist. Data as to the cause of death, and the mental and physical maladies of each individual, will, for the benefit of those who come after him, be registered as rigorously as births, deaths, and marriages are at present registered; and each family will keep its records as jealously as some now keep their family tree.

When that time comes, and when the great but, as I have said, comparatively neglected science of heredity—the science which, more than any other, teaches the lesson of a large and loving charity, and impresses every thoughtful inquirer with the futility and presumption of any human creature pronouncing final judgment upon another—receives the attention it demands; when the mind will be treated in connection with the body, and the body in connection with the mind; and when medicine and religion either collaborate or are combined in one profession—the secret of the inconsistencies of such souls as Heine may perhaps be understood.

Till that time come, and in the absence of the necessary data, the question of what I may call the plurality of Heine's personality is one which I must only raise to leave, contenting myself by calling attention to a passage in his works which seems to indicate that Heine himself was conscious of this plural personality :—

"I am a Jew, I am a Christian," he says ; "I am tragedy, I am comedy—Heraclitus and Democritus in one ; a Greek, a Hebrew ; an adorer of despotism as incarnate in Napoleon, an admirer of communism embodied in Proudhon ; a Latin, a Teuton ; a beast, a devil, a god !"

If there is, however, one thing which to the student of Heine's character seems certain, it is that the secret of much of his misery lay in the fact that he was a moral coward—a man who persistently and deliberately turned away from the obligations which duty imposed when those obligations clashed with his personal comfort or his inclinations. "Alas!" he said once in a jest which had a pitiful kernel of earnest, "alas! mental torture is easier to be borne than physical pain; and were I offered the alternative between a bad conscience and an aching tooth, I should choose the former."

Like all men of his class, Heine brought upon himself by his cowardice far greater sufferings than those from which he shrank. His wrong-doing gave him no peace. Every duty he sought to evade came back to him at last with its demands but the heavier for the delay; every evil action recoiled upon himself. He was the most unlucky of sinners, and he once said that if there fell from the sky a shower of crown-pieces he should bring home only a broken pate, while others gathered silver manna. Nor was he any happier in his selfish seeking after ease of mind, for not all his callousness and casuistry could still the voice of conscience. None knew better than Heine the dignity and beauty of purity, and to none did honour and purity speak in more imploring tones. In his verses " To a Child " he says :—

> "Oh! thou árt like a flower;
>   So fair, so pure, thou art;
>   I look on thee, and sorrow
>   Lies heavy on my heart.
>   My hand upon thy head
>   I fain would gently lay,
>   Praying that God may keep thee thus,
>   Flowerlike and pure alway."

It is hard to believe that these lines were written by a heartless profligate. They come, no doubt, from a sin-stained nature ; yet is there not to be heard in them some crying out of the man's soul for the purity he had lost—purity which he seemed to see gazing

out at him with mournful, mute reproach
from the depths of the child eyes into which
he looked?

And there is another saying of his which
reminds us that Heine's good angel never
quite deserted him, and in which we hear
her sorrowful cry at the wreck of so noble
a soul :—

"It is not merely what we have done," he
says, "not merely the posthumous fruit of
our activity which entitles us to honour-
able recognition after death, but also our
striving itself, and especially our unsuccessful striving—the shipwrecked, fruitless, but
great-souled *Will* to do!"

Amid all the noisome mists which darken
Heine's life we catch at times a glimpse as
of the upward beating of broken pinions;

just as between the chinks in the armour of cynicism and satire in which he thought fit to array himself, we hear, at intervals, the beating of a sensitive human heart.

And, indeed, one is tempted to think sometimes of Heine, that in him Nature intended to create a spiritual and intellectual giant who should astonish the world by the daring of his genius, a being in whom she wished to display to all men the infinite and varied profusion of her resources; as if she had therefore, in pursuance of this plan, bestowed on him a double share of the qualities which go to constitute a human soul, but that—before she had time to blend and interweave these qualities into a balanced and perfected whole—some evil spirit had snatched her unfinished work from her hand, and cast it forth, a medley of wild virtues and wilder vices, into the world.

What Heine lacked physically, mentally, and morally was—as his brilliant country-woman, the late Emma Lazarus, has pointed out—health. And as we look back upon his life—a life splendid in the possibility of what might have been, but pitiful in view of what was; a life which, though it lies like an unsuccessful battle-field, dark-strewn with shameful corpses before us, is yet not all unlighted by the beacon-fire of knightly deed and noble word—the strange question which, in the restless searching of his spirit, Heine once asked himself, rises to our mind—"Can it be possible that genius, like the pearl in the oyster, is, after all, only a splendid disease?"

With that question let us end this paper. An unsatisfactory ending, perhaps ; but an unanswered question is, after all, the fitting and only close to a paper which seeks to deal with the personality of Heinrich Heine.

A NOTE ON ROSSETTI.

TO DANTE GABRIEL ROSSETTI.

THOU knew'st that island, far away and lone,
   Whose shores are as a harp where billows break
   In spray of music, and the breezes shake
O'er spicy seas a woof of colour and tone,
While that sweet music echoes like a moan
   In the island's heart, and sighs around the lake,
   Where, watching fearfully a watchful snake,
A damsel weeps upon her emerald throne.

Life's ocean, breaking round thy senses' shore,
   Struck golden song, as from the strand of day :
   For us the joy, for thee the fell foe lay—
Pain's blinking snake around the fair isle's core,
   Turning to sighs the enchanted sounds that play
Around thy lovely island evermore.

THEODORE WATTS.

A NOTE ON ROSSETTI.

I.

"I GRUDGE Wordsworth every vote he gets," said Rossetti once to Mr. Hall Caine, and the remark is significant. Wordsworth and Rossetti stand at opposite poles of poetic and personal individuality. The one is as distinctively the poet of the open air and the hillside, as the other is of the studio and the study. Wordsworth's work has a background of sky and mountain, and his verse is blown through as by a

E

breeze from hill-summits. There are passages in his poems in which Nature speaks to us as intimately as she speaks in the rippling, running tinkling of the brooklet over its pebbly bed.

To the artist who is truly in sympathy with her, Nature's voice is audible in the study or studio, as well as on the mountain or in the fields. The lyric which, like the sound of bells borne from a distance, comes and goes in his brain during his secluded moments, is but the continuation of the song the wind sang to him when it rustled among the dry reeds on the river's marge; or was called into being by the gleam of blue sky, framed in between rain-beaten and glistening tree-tops, which caught his eye in his morning walk. And when he returns to the mountain and fields, he does not leave his art behind him as something which would there be out of place. On the contrary, the sonnet which rises involuntarily to his lips is as much a part of the land-scape at which he gazes, as is the lustre of red sorrel that darkens the hillside to burnished copper, or as the tawny gold of withered leaves on a clump of autumnal beeches. Hence there are poems by Wordsworth of which it may be said that, to a sympathetic reader, suns seem to rise and set in the verses, stars to sparkle be-tween the lines, and the scent of blossoming clover-fields to exhale from the pages. It is not Art but Nature which lends such magic to his lines. Viewed apart from their marvellous interpretation of the great

Mother, many of them are cold and colour-
less, and lack the passion and the sensuous beauty which are characteristics of
Rossetti's work.   To pass from *The Ex-
cursion* to *The House of Life* is like turning
aside from the white sunlight and crystalline
freshness of a spring morning into the
seclusion of some temple of a bygone age.
Outside the heart beat high and the blood
ran swiftly under the exhilaration born of
broad sky-spaces and windy meadows, but
here there is no glad . burst of morning
sunlight to greet us, and the perfumed air,
sweet almost to oppressiveness, hangs hot
and heavy like a curtain.   Is it within the
precincts of a Catholic sanctuary we are
standing ? Shadow-shrouded aisles, sensuous
music, and the serene splendour of jewelled

panes!—surely these are the surroundings
we associate with the emotional religion of
the South! And yet something there is
in the scene which reminds us less of the
Christian cloister than of the pagan temple,
more of the worship of Venus than of the
Virgin; for, through the clouds of wreathing
incense, we see white arms outstretched
wooingly towards us, above the billowy ebb
and flow, the stormy rising and falling of
whiter bosoms. And then the music dies
away, the poem is ended, and, all drowsy-
eyed and slumber-steeped, we waken to real
life again, like men who have been rudely
aroused from some drug-born but delicious
dream of an Oriental paradise.

That the super-sensuousness and Southern
warmth of colouring, which are so frequent

in Rossetti's work, should have caused
readers, who imperfectly understand the
passionate nature of the man and the sym-
bolism that appealed so powerfully to his
nature, to take exception to the voluptuous-
ness of his language, is not surprising. But
he held, and held strongly, that the non-
sensuous can best be apprehended by means
of an image dealing with the sensuous;
and he would have contended that—instead
of sticking fast at the sensuous image, and
seeing in it only "fleshliness"—those who
read his poetry aright, see through and
beyond the sensuous image, to the non-
sensuous which it typifies. And to Rossetti,
whose whole nature was dominated by his
artistic instincts, Art was in and of herself,
and apart from every other consideration,

pure, sacred, and inviolate; and he was shocked (the word is not too strong) to find that what in his eyes was but a faithfully-finished and harmonious work of art, was regarded by others as wanting in delicacy and in discretion.

That his poems are always healthy, not even his most enthusiastic admirers will insist. There are passages which are heavy with an overpowering sweetness as of many hyacinths. The atmosphere is like that of a hothouse, in which, amid all the odorous deliciousness, we gasp for a breath of outer air again. And in some of his work, self-consciousness is so painfully present as to remind us of the line in his sonnet, "Willow-wood"—

"And pity of self through all made broken moan."

"What is it," we are moved to say to ourselves as we read—"what is it, after all, that such a hullaballoo is made about? Is this the expression of genuine and unexaggerated feeling? or is it morbid self-consciousness?" Nor are we altogether certain, as we lay down the book, to which question the answer should be in the affirmative.

II.

WE live now-a-days at so rapid a pace, that many people regard their occasional dips into Literature and into Art in the same way that they regard a meal snatched hastily during the "five-minutes wait" on a long journey, when each traveller looks out—not for the fare which is best worth having, but for that which can be quickly disposed of, and with the least expenditure of personal trouble. As a consequence, not a few commercially-minded craftsmen have come to consider "marketability" before merit, aiming, tradesmen-like, at effect instead of at thoroughness, at popularity instead of at perfection. Nor do they forget, when laying out their goods to advantage, to cast certain sidelong glances upon the folk for whom these goods are intended, in order that their literary or artistic "show counter" may not be wanting in the articles likely to please that whimsical, novelty-loving, but promptly-paying customer, the public.

Not thus did Rossetti accommodate himself to the requirements of the times. He was "in" the nineteenth century but not "of" it; and his presence among us in these latter days was in many respects an anachronism.

He was the posthumous son of an age long since passed away—a literary and artistic Rip Van Winkle, who was for ever harking back with the tenderest reminiscences to that vanished Mediævalism with which, in taste and sympathy, he was so thoroughly at one.

He had no wish to catch the public vote; and popular, in the sense of being read and appreciated by the multitude—which looks first at the sentiment, and secondly, and often indifferently, at the form in which that sentiment is expressed—his work will never be. It is too purely artistic to appeal to those who are incapable of appreciating a work of art on its artistic merits; and if one were to read a score of the *House of Life* sonnets to a popular entertainment audience, two-thirds of those present would consider the selection peculiarly and per-plexingly dull, and would probably go away with the remark that they "had not been educated up to it," which, on the whole, would be a tolerably correct statement of the case. There is no "playing to the gods" in any single poem of Rossetti's. All that he does he does thoroughly. Some of his sonnets remind us of Oriental ivory work, in which every available inch and corner has been used for ornamental purposes, and in which, too, among the multiplicity of minor decorations, we find it difficult to distinguish the original design. They are finished now and then to faultiness, and would gain rather than lose were they a trifle harsher and ruder,—were they more evidently the outcome of impulse and spontaneity, and less suggestive of the dexterity of the craftsman. That he must have taken infinite pains with them is certain, for they have been tuned and retuned to concert pitch. Every consonant has been considered in connection with the consonant which precedes or follows it, and each vowel has been calculated to a nicety. As musical compositions they are unique. There is fascination in the mere sound of them, independently of their meaning. And, indeed, all Rossetti's work is noticeable for its confluent volume of sound,

and rhythmic splendour and sonority, but
to attain this, he is occasionally guilty of
making sense subservient to sound, as ex-
emplified in the third line of the sonnet,
" Through Death to Love " :—

> " Like labour-laden moon-clouds faint to flee
>   From winds that sweep the winter-bitten wold,—
>   Like multiform circumfluence manifold
> Of night's flood-tide," etc.,

in which, "like multiform circumfluence
manifold" is apparently introduced, less on
account of its descriptive or imaginative
significance, than for the sake of an unusual
combination of alliterative sounds. But it
was only rarely that Rossetti allowed his
rapturous and exultant delight in sweet
and sonorous measures to interfere with his
otherwise analytical attention to perspicuity
and logical relationship, for in his most

passionate inspirations he was not too absorbed to cast an occasional sidelong glance
at that standard of "fundamental brain-
work" which he held to be the very first
consideration of Art.

III.

THE reasonableness of the complaints of
those who take exception to Rossetti's work
on the score of its "lusciousness," we, who
admire his poetry most, may and must admit.
But what we do not admit as reasonable
are the strictures passed by the folk who
complain that the sole aim of his work is
to gratify the artistic perceptions and to
charm the senses,—that he has nothing to
teach them, and that they search in vain

among his poems for religious or moral
instruction. " Is this all ? " they say with
outstretched palms of protest, lugubrious
countenances, and a general air of injured
probity, not altogether unlike that of a cab-
man who has received sixpence over and
above his legitimate fare—"is this all, then,
that Mr. Rossetti has to tell us ? " Now,
though no-one will deny that the influence
of the highest art is, directly or indirectly,
ethical, it is not for that reason the bounden
duty of every artist to pose as a moralist.
The folk who can call nothing good, unless
it carry, dog-like, at its tail a tin-can of
noisy and rattling morality, and the critics
who—forgetting that the very over-weight-
ing of individuality, genius, as we call it,
which gives a man such power on one

side and in one direction, necessitates, by natural and inevitable law, a corresponding under-balance on the other—cannot award their grudging meed of praise for honest work done, without complaining that something else has been left undone, are a thankless set. After Carlyle had devoted his life to labour little better than slavery, that he might write a *Frederick the Great* or a *French Revolution*, and in so doing had injured his general health and digestion (and, consequently, his temper), they fell to abusing him for his irritability in what is, after all, no affair of theirs in any way—his private and domestic life. And after Rossetti, one of the most original interpreters and creators of the beautiful, in two separate but kindred realms of art, since the days of Michel Angelo, had with infinite pain and spirit-travail (pain and travail with which, as he himself said, his "very life ebbed out") succeeded in producing some of the most exquisite poems in the language, as well as many unique pictures, they reproached him because they failed to find in his work the evidence of a purpose for which he never intended it—the inculcation of moral or religious truth.

That he was neither the discoverer of a new star in our philosophical heavens, nor the propounder of a theory for the social or moral amelioration of the race, is undeniable, for to be either the one or the other was never at any time his aim. He was a man of meditative rather than of speculative order of mind, somewhat narrow in tastes and sympathies, and far too absorbed in the contemplation of his own many-hued moods and emotions to trouble himself much about those of his fellow-creatures who had no part to play in the all-important *rôle* of ministering to his overmastering and ex- quisitely-developed sense of beauty. Art was his supreme mistress, and he served her long and faithfully. It was as an artist only that he claimed to be judged ; and whether we approve or regret his choice, we have no right to demand that any man of genius, be he preacher, painter, or poet, shall be all things to all men. On the contrary, we must accept with gladness the good things he gives us, and seek elsewhere for the spiritual or intellectual gifts which he cannot and does not pretend to bestow.

A SINGER FROM OVER SEAS.

A SINGER FROM OVER SEAS.

I.

WHEN, about a hundred odd years ago, there was a split in the big firm of England and Company, and one of the most enter-prising of the younger members decided to set up a separate establishment, giving notice that she had " no connection with the firm on the other side of the water," there were, of course, a great many posts in the filling up of which some difficulty was experienced ; and it is only within recent years that America has found her representative woman-poet. That there are many American women whose verse is excellent, is undeniable ; but the fact that, with the exception of Mrs. S. M. B. Piatt, there is only one, who may be. said to have a public of her own on this side of the Atlantic, is significant, when we remember the popularity of Longfellow, Whittier, Lowell, and other singers of the sterner sex.

The woman-poet in question is, of course, Louise Chandler Moulton, and as new editions of her two volumes, *Swallowflights* and *In the Garden of Dreams*, have recently been issued in this country by Messrs. Macmillan and Co., a consideration of her claims as a poet is likely to be of interest to English readers.

Nearly every minor poet who publishes now-a-days a slender volume of verse, seems to think that the door of his or her house of song must not be thrown open to the world until there has been erected at the entrance —like a stuccoed portico set in front of a suburban villa—a lengthy narrative-poem or "epic." But one takes up Mrs. Moulton's volumes with none the less pleasure for the fact that all her poems consist of sonnets and lyrics. Short her flights of song may be, but they are musical, and marked by exquisite beauty of imagery and diction, as will be seen by the following verses from "The House of Death," a poem which is not unworthy of being ranked with the work of Mrs. Browning and Miss Rossetti—our two supreme and pre-eminent women-poets,

whose sacred presence one would scarcely
venture to profane by the suggestion of a
possible third. The beauty of expression
and of poetic imagery in the lines I have
italicised, and the skilful way in which the
music is made to deepen in the third verse,
are very noticeable.

> "Not a hand has lifted the latchet,
>   Since she went out of the door;
> No footstep shall cross the threshold,
>   Since she can come in no more.
>
> "There is rust upon locks and hinges,
>   And mould and blight on the walls,
> *And silence faints in the chambers,*
>   *And darkness waits in the halls,—*
>
> "Waits as all things have waited,
>   Since she went that day of spring,
> Borne in her pallid splendour,
>   To dwell in the Court of the King;
>
> "With lilies on brow and bosom,
>   With robes of silken sheen,
> *And her wonderful frozen beauty,*
>   *The lilies and silk between.*"

This poem is from *Swallowflights*, Mrs. Moulton's first volume. In her second, *In the Garden of Dreams*, there is a lyric of great dignity and beauty entitled " The Strength of the Hills." It opens by describing " the old brown house " where the singer passed her childhood, and then goes on to tell of the " great hills " which rose " silent and steadfast and gloomy and grey " in the distance, and of her childish dreams concerning them. Here are the two concluding verses :—

" But calm in the distance the great hills rose,
　　Deaf unto rapture and dumb unto pain,
　Since they knew that Joy is the mother of Grief,
　And remembered a butterfly's life is brief,
　　And the sun sets only to rise again.

" They will brood and dream and be silent as now,
　　When the youngest children alive to-day

"Have grown to be women and men—grown old,
And gone from the world like a tale that is told,
And even whose echo forgets to stay."

It seems ungracious to find fault after reading such exquisite lyrics as these; but one cannot help wishing sometimes that Mrs. Moulton had a keener sense of humour, or perhaps I should say a keener sense of the humorous associations which become connected with certain words. Separated by a few pages from "The Strength of the Hills," I find in her *Garden of Dreams* a poem which is spoilt by a word. It bears the singularly unhappy title of "Old Jones is dead"—a title more suggestive of a publication with the imprint of Messrs. Moore and Burgess than of Messrs. Macmillan and Co.

This is probably the one and only lyric in the language in which the name "Jones" is used seriously; and to say that Mrs. Moulton has succeeded in dignifying that unimpressive appellation is to pay no small compliment to her skill. She tells us that, when sitting at her window, she heard one passer-by inform another that an old man, unknown to her, was dead; and in her deliberate choice of the name "Jones" for the dead man upon whose fate she is speculating, she lends the poem something of human and everyday pathos. But I wish she could have avoided asking if "Jones"—mentioning him by name—were "one with the stars in the watching sky."

"But I sat and pondered what it might mean,
Thus to be dead while the world went by:

Did Jones see farther than we have seen?
   Was he one with the stars in the watching sky?
Or down there under the growing grass
Does he hear the feet of the daylight pass?

     *   *   *   *   *   *

Does he brood in the long night under the sod,
   On the joys and sorrows he used to know;
Or far in some wonderful world of God,
   Where the shining seraphs stand row on row,
Does he wake like a child at the daylight's gleam,
And know that the past was a night's short dream?

Is he dead, and a clod there, down below;
   Or dead and wiser than any alive;
Which? Ah, who of us all may know?
   Or who can say how the dead folk thrive?
But the summer morning is cool and sweet,
And I hear the live folk laugh in the street."

The second of these verses is fine, and the
way in which the poet's thoughts turn, in
the concluding couplet, from the man who is
lying dead to the laughter of the " live folk "
in the street and to the sweetness of the
summer morning, is in its very triviality
impressive.

Mrs. Moulton's sonnets are admitted to be among the best, if, indeed, they are not the best, which America has produced. " It seems to me," said Whittier once of her work, " that the sonnet was never set to such music, and never weighted with more deep and tender thought"; and, as far back as 1878, when she had only published a single slender volume of poems, the late Professor Minto wrote of her that he "did not know where to find, among the works of English poetesses, the same self-controlled fulness of expression with the same depth and tenderness of simple feeling," adding that the following sonnet, " One Dread," might have been penned by Sir Philip Sidney :—

"No depth, dear Love, for thee is too profound;
 There is no farthest height thou may'st not dare,
 Nor shall thy wings fail in the upper air:
In funeral robe and wreath my past lies bound;
No old-time voice assails me with its sound
 When thine I hear; no former joy seems fair;
 And now one only thing could bring despair,
One grief, like compassing seas, my life surround,
 One only terror in my way be met,
One great eclipse change my glad day to night,
One phantom only turn from red to white
 The lips whereon thy lips have once been set:
Thou knowest well, dear Love, what that must be—
The dread of some dark day unshared by thee."

As an instance of Mrs. Moulton's vigour of description I will quote the octave of the sonnet "At Sea" :—

"Outside the mad sea ravens for its prey,
 Shut from it by a floating plank I lie;
 Through this round window search the faithless sky,
The hungry waves that fain would rend and slay;
The live-long, blank, interminable way,
 Blind with the sun and hoarse with the wind's cry
 Of wild, unconquerable mutiny,
Until night comes more terrible than day."

The lines I have italicised are really fine, and the whole sonnet conveys such sense of space, and pictures such waste of hurrying, heaving waters, that, as one reads, one seems listening to the wild uproar of wind and wave, to hear the salt blast whistling through the rigging, and to feel it sting and buffet the cheek with the flying spray.

II.

THERE is much that is tragic in the in evitable conditions under which each of us is born, but few things in life are more tragic. than the ease with which human beings forget life's tragedy. To find ourselves in this world, understanding little of whence we came, and less of whither we go; to love and to be loved infinitely, knowing that, sooner or later, we and our loved ones must part, and that Death, like the slowly-contracting walls of the Inquisition, is day by day closing in upon us, and upon those we love—all this is so infinitely pathetic that one's only wonder is that so few of the actors who strut their little hour upon the theatre of life should play the part of Hamlet. It is because she can never for long forget that for each of us there will dawn a day when over the magic mirror of our eyes the film of death will steal; when the fleeting phantasmagoria of sea and sky will no longer be reflected from the mirror's dull and glazing surface; and when the eager, anxious brain will be a decaying pulp of grey and sodden matter,—that Mrs.

Moulton's work is so frequently marked by a note of melancholy. But hers is a sadness which is always sincere, and is in no way related to the Byronic melancholy of the *poseur* and the sentimentalist. It is the sadness of one who is supremely conscious of the tragedy of life and death. Her fairest flowers of song are woven for a funeral wreath ; her pages are hung thick with *immortelles ;* and in her nightingale-haunted *Garden of Dreams*, the sombre cypress grows side by side with the lily and the rose.

Physical fear of death and horror of its loneliness have done much to sadden her nature, and consequently her poetry. " I long so unutterably," she once said, " that some one dear to me might die when I

G

die, that so we might bear each other company in that awful loneliness at the very
thought of which I shudder."

To her it seems as if death were not
natural, but unnatural; as if it were some
dreadful mistake which God has made; a
mistake which He will surely discover and
set right before long. As if it were
scarcely less natural to tear a nestling babe
from the bosom of its mother and to cast
it out into the night, than to drag us from
the familiar breast of this earth to which
we cling—this earth with its love and friendship and little children, its fields and flowers,
sea and sky, sunshine and starlight, and
sweet consolations of Art and Song—and
hustle us away underground, thick-walled
in a desolate dungeon of oozy clay, where

never a ray of daylight can reach us more, nor human voice break the black horror that wraps us round.

To her, therefore, there is some hint of sadness in the joyous gladness of June sunshine—some memory of the Junes that are no more, some anticipation of the winters that are to be :—

"O June, fair queen of sunshine and of flowers,
The affluent year will hold you not again!
Once, only once, can youth and love be ours,
And after them the autumn and the rain."

III.

MRS. MOULTON, herself, will not admit that her poems are more melancholy than those of her sister singers, and I remember that on one occasion when the subject was being discussed, she instanced as evidence to the contrary the following *rondeau*, " The Old Beau " :—

"He was a gay deceiver when
    The century was young, they say,
And triumphed over other men,
    And wooed the girls, and had his way.

No maiden ever said him nay,
    No rival ever crossed him then,
    And painters vied to paint him when
The century was young, they say.

Now the new dogs must have their day;
    And the old beau has found that when
He pleads, things go another way,
    And lonely 'mong the younger men,
    He hears their heartless laughter when
He boasts about that other day."

That this has a certain lightness of touch, and, as an experiment in an old French form, is entirely successful, none will deny. But even in these sprightly verses is there not some suggestion of pathos in the reference to the vain and unvenerated old age of the lonely beau, who has outlived his own generation, and, like a spectral moon when the sun is high, lingers on, the living ghost of a vanished past?

No one who looks upon life with earnest eyes can fail to be touched by the passionate human cry which rings from Mrs. Moulton's poems. No one whose ear is attuned to catch the wail that is to be heard in the maddest, merriest music of the violin, to whom the sound of wind and sea at midnight is like that of innumerable lamentations; no one who, in the movement of a multitude of human beings — be that multitude marching to the bounding music of fife and drum, or hurrying to witness a meeting of the starving Unemployed—no one who in all these hears something of "the still, sad music of humanity" can read her verses unstirred. It is more than probable, too, that the note of melancholy, which is so frequent in Mrs. Moulton's poems, may by many readers be counted a singular and constant charm; but, on the other hand, it cannot be denied that it has tended to limit her intellectual range. In the House of the Muse there are many mansions; and the poet who, like Shakespeare, writes for all times and all men—who sweeps the whole gamut of human emotion—sits not always in the darkened room wherein Sorrow lies weeping, but seeks also the sunny upper-chamber, where Sorrow's twin sister Joy dances and sings. Gladness should have its place in poetry no less than grief. The lark's song is not unmusical because of its lightheartedness, the laughter of children is more melodious than their sobbing, and the secret even of the nightingale's singing is not sorrow but joy. Of course the beautiful and much-quoted line of Shelley's about "sweetest songs" and "saddest thought," will inevitably rise like an unquiet and unlaid ghost to rebuke me, but is it not nearly time we gave that weary line a rest? Byron and certain poets of his school caught the mental "mumps" in their youth ("mumps" is not a pretty word nor poetic, but it is the word which carries my meaning best), and did what they could to communicate the disease, which is contagious, to English poetry. To what extent they failed or succeeded need not here be discussed; but the fact that they went about with their faces wrapped in flannel is no reason why subsequent poets should follow their example.

If sweetness cannot be attained except by sickliness, then sweetness must go, if only that we may gain in strength. There is a sweetness which palls and cloys, a sweetness which recalls the story of the woman who, after she had been living for some days in an orangery, said that she grew at last to long for the pungent smell of the stables. The sweetness of Shakespeare, Wordsworth, and Milton—all sane men and sound—was not of this heavy-odoured, hot-house, and enervating description. Their harps were strung with iron chords, and theirs was the bracing sweetness of the sea-breeze.

I do not for a moment mean to imply

by all this, that any trace of sickliness is to be found in Mrs. Moulton's verse, but I believe that had she communed less with the "ghosts" (the word literally "haunts" her volumes) of dead friends and of dead days—had she swept a wider mental horizon, and been less introspective—the beauty of her imagery, her lyric grace, and the general excellence of her technique, would have entitled her to take place with the major, instead of with the minor singers of her sex.

As it is, she is admitted to be the first woman-poet of America; but in years to come she will be remembered as the writer of many exquisite sonnets and of some lyrics, which, in the shuddering intensity of their passionate cry and protest against death, are

unique among the work of woman-poets.
Of such lyrics, the following is one of the
most characteristic :—

"You have made this world so dear,
How can I go forth alone,
In the barque that phantoms steer,
To a port afar and unknown?

The desperate Mob of the Dead—
Will they hustle me to and fro,
Or leave me alone to tread
The path of my desolate woe?

Shall I shriek with terror and pain
For the death that I cannot die?
And pray with a longing vain
To the gods that mock my cry?

Oh, hold me closer, my dear!
Strong is your clasp—aye, strong;
But stronger the touch that I fear,
And the darkness to come is long!"

Sombre and even terrible in its intensity
this lurid picture of " the desperate Mob of
the Dead" may be; but to us who believe

that there is even now raging such battle between Life and Death as that "war in heaven" of which John Milton sang to us, it is not without a whisper of hope. For even as then Satan and his hosts were beaten back and cast out by the God-led legions of light, so we believe that there will come a time when Life shall be all-triumphant, and when, in the magnificent words of Mr. Swinburne—

"As a god self-slain on his own strange altar,
Death lies dead."

And even though we had no such hope or belief, these terrible lines are not without their message; for the recognition of the awful mystery which hangs over each of us, should surely knit human creature to human creature in a common bond of fellowship and love. Even for the man with whom we have otherwise no sympathy, or who, it may be, has done us a grievous wrong, we can entertain nothing but pitying tenderness. " Thou, too, hast soon to leave thy loved ones, and to go out and alone into the darkness from which I shrink," we say to ourselves, as we think of the insignificance of his enmity. " Let me, then, help rather than harm thee, while yet thou and I are here ! "

ROBERTSON OF BRIGHTON:

THE MAN AND HIS MOODS.

ROBERTSON OF BRIGHTON:

THE MAN AND HIS MOODS.

I.

FREDERICK WILLIAM ROBERTSON—"the greatest preacher of the century," according to the late Dean Stanley—has been dead more than forty years; but to us who read his sermons to-day it seems as if, under the cold clods of that cemetery near the sea at Brighton, a human heart must be beating still, and sending out warm pulsing waves of life through the veins of this ageing world. For his sermons strike home alike to heart and head as sermons rarely do. They make us feel that it is for us and no other that their message is intended. There is no evading the unpleasant truth by generalizing, or by mentally reviewing the heads of our friends and acquaintances for one to whom to pass the cap. " Thou art the man," is their message to the reader. He is isolated. He is summoned against his will to the bar of conscience, for Robertson's aim was, as he often said, that his sermons should be "felt," not that they should be "admired." They are no easy-chair elaborations, leisurely dotted down by the aid of commentary and concordance. On the contrary, he so threw himself into his work that his very words are instinct with his own personality, and each sentence is, as it were, a spending of himself. He had a wonderful capability for concentration of energy. Study him as we will, in his public or in his private life, in society or in solitude, this feature of his character—and it is a feature which in itself goes far to lend power and purpose to any man's work—is everywhere noticeable. His very manner of walking was marked by it. There was no sauntering, loitering, or turning aside in pursuit of whim or fancy. He pressed eagerly onward, as if goaded by an invisible hand, but, for all his haste, letting nothing pass by unnoticed. Even when starting for a walk, he set out generally with some purpose or destination in view; and no matter what time lay at his disposal, he could brook no delay, but chose the straightest road, and followed it closely in spite of obstacles. When on horseback he would clear hedge, ditch, or wall, rather than lose five minutes in search of a gate ; and when he set out, gun in hand, for a day's shooting, he threw himself with such ardour into the sport, that he could spare no time to eat, to drink, or to rest, but pressed impetuously on, until nightfall compelled him to return home, famished and spent.

By this singleness of purpose and concentration of energy, the preparation of Robertson's sermons was equally marked. Every nerve in his body, as well as his intellectual faculties, was at work ; his heart beat faster, his breathing became quicker, and his very limbs seemed in some way to lend themselves to the task. Had he been less impatient, less feverish and impetuous, his life and his life's work might have been lengthened by many years; but into whatever he undertook, and most of all into his sermons, he threw himself with an enthusiasm which was a consuming fire within him,—which literally burnt his vitality and his strength away. "I am not fit for ministerial work," he once wrote to a friend; "I want years and years to calm me. My heart is too feverish—quivers and throbs too much as flesh recently cut by the surgeon's knife."

But of himself he thought never, of his work always; and Miss Olive Schreiner's beautiful allegory about the painter whose pictures had a wonderful wealth and richness of colouring, the secret of which none could discover, until, after his death, there

was found, under his heart, a wound whence
the red life-blood had been drained, might
have been written in all sincerity about the
sermons of Frederick Robertson—the sermons which we settle down cosily to read,
on the Sunday afternoons when we have
dined well, and wish to feel on as good
terms with the next world as with this.

———————

II.

"Every man," says Mr. Lowell, in his
article on Rousseau, "is conscious that he
leads two lives,—the one trivial and ordinary, the other sacred and recluse; one
which he carries to society and the dinner-
table, the other in which his youth and

aspiration survive for him, and which is a confidence between himself and God. Both may be equally sincere, and there need be no contradiction between them, any more than in a healthy man between soul and body."

This is the utterance, not of one with a low ideal, but of one whose feelings upon the subject of the higher life were in no sense morbid; of a man who recognized that God has made us human, not angelic; that He does not wish us to deepen one side of our nature by stultifying the other. Mr. Lowell was essentially "sane," and so too was Frederick Robertson — except when dealing with questions that pertained to himself. Generous to a fault in his judgment of others, for himself he had no charity. He was conscious of the two existences of which Mr. Lowell speaks, but could not reconcile himself to the lower. He strove to keep his spiritual nature ever and always at "concert pitch," and came to regard as culpable and weak the failure which must inevitably attend such effort. His spirituality was too intense. It was nothing less than a disease, and, in a worldly sense, a calamity. The atmosphere in which he lived was so ethereal, his thoughts and aspirations so habitually high, that he became impatient of all human weakness, and felt that he had been untrue to himself, and to his conscience, because he could not sustain in the commonplace intercourse of daily life the condition of feeling which these thoughts and aspirations aroused.

Hence his life was one long-continued struggle and unrest. A divine discontent was ever his, and he writes in his diary of feeling "sad and dispirited" at the thought of his own "utter uselessness," and of being constantly overwhelmed with a sense of "defeat." "Our defeats," says Jean Paul Richter, "are not far removed from our victories"; and to no one are these words more applicable than to Robertson of Brighton.

This tendency to self-depreciation meets us continually in our study of the great preacher, but allowance must always be made, for the exaggeration of feeling to which his intense susceptibility to the mood of the moment rendered him peculiarily liable, and in which lay the secret of much of his misery.

Was Robertson's whole being lending itself to the contemplation of the unseen world, this impressionability would bear him, as on wings, to a region when the earth and the earth-life seemed but a dream-delusion, and eternity the only reality.

But there were moments, as there must be in the life of all who are human beings and not glorified spirits, when Robertson's emotions were dull and cold, and his thoughts leaden-winged and earthy;—moments when God drew back, and the world drew near, and the lower nature within him, impatient of the stern control so long maintained upon it, cried out with hungry longing for a life less joyless and chill. At such moments, this same impressionability would shut out the spiritual world as by a screen, and, by intensifying the mood of the moment, would lend to this world, and to the things of this world, a glamour, more seductive, perhaps, than that which they wore to the eyes of the worldling; and was thus the very traitor within the citadel that sought to throw open the gates to the enemy.

The grosser pleasures which appeal to the ordinary human animal, Robertson found it no hard matter to forego. But for the things of the sensuous life—Art with her purity and power; Poetry with her passion and peace; and Music which, as he hung in rapt ecstasy upon the "linked sweetness long drawn out" of symphony or sonata, set his sound-intoxicated spirit quivering like thin flame— for these he had a love and a longing which to his overstrained spirituality seemed un-

worthy in one who was toiling in spirit up
the steep ascent of Calvary. It was only
for himself, however, as has been said, that
he set this unnatural standard. For other
people he made every allowance; and even
in regard to that which is forbidden, he
more than once pointed out that sin lies
in the indulgence, not in the rising of desire.
· And if he did not hold, like Richard Jefferies,
that "the ascetics are the only impure,"
Robertson was as far removed from preach-
ing asceticism, as was the author of *The
Story of My Heart.* That much of his
morbidness of self-judgment, and of his
frequent depression of spirits, were due to
advancing sickness and other physical causes,
is certain. In his healthier hours he had
the light heart and high spirits of a child,—

to illustrate which I cannot do better than quote from Mr. Stopford Brooke's *Life and Letters of Frederick William Robertson*, a letter to Mr. Brooke, penned by one who knew Robertson personally :—

"His gracious manner and winning courtesy I shall not easily forget," writes Mr. Brooke's correspondent. "I recall the first day I met him as vividly as if it were yesterday—the serious smile of welcome, the questioning look from his eyes, the frankly offered hand. We walked up a hill commanding a noble view of sea and mountain. His face lit up—he drank in with a deep breath the wide landscape. The contrast of the white foam dashing on a beach of blue slate pebbles—the racing of the scattering and fitful breezes upon the sea

—the purple of the distant hills, were all marked by him with loving observation. He was happy in pointing out the delicacy of the clouds which an upper current was combing out upon the sky. He stooped to gather the wild daffodils which were tossing in the wind. Nothing was lost upon him He touched all the points of the scene clearly enough to instruct his listeners how to see them, but with such poetic tact that he did not injure what I may call the sensibility of nature. One thought more, that is, of the loveliness he spoke of than of the speaker: it was the unconscious art of genius."

Here we have Robertson as he was apart from the disease which darkened his mind and warped his self-judgment. How heartily he hated gloom may be seen from a passage in one of his letters: "A sunny, cheerful view of life, resting on truth and fact, co-existing with practical aspiration ever to make things, men, and self better than they are—*that* I believe is the true healthful poetry of existence." The sadness which overshadowed him so constantly was the sadness which the author of *Festus* calls "the ground of all great thoughts" —never the melancholy of the misanthrope. It was not far removed perhaps from that "remorse of conscience for *future* actions" which Jean Paul curiously says, "can spoil some good men's enjoyment of life." And in one respect Robertson's unceasing watchfulness of himself, and his terror of becoming a sentimentalist and a dreamer—a man who wrote and said fine things, but was incapable of ordering his life accordingly—were not so superfluous as might be imagined. The self-delusion which makes "the conscience dreamy with the anodyne of lofty thought, while the life is grovelling and sensual," is the most fatal of the many pitfalls which beset the feet of the man of emotional and poetic temperament. It is such a conscience-soothing, soul-benumbing delusion that it works his ruin even while he thinks it his surest salvation. It comes to him with its harlot beauty draped in the robes of an angel of light, and sings hymns before the very gates of hell; and it bids him close his eyes in prayer, that it may set his unsuspecting feet upon the high-road that leads to destruction. But Robertson was one of those whose weakness, recognized as weakness, and guarded against, becomes strength. He knew the danger which lay in the almost womanly intensity of his emotions; and would have none of that feeble and frothy sentiment which dies with the moment which calls it forth. The feelings which did not find their fitting outcome in action, the thought which did not take form in a thing, but fell to earth again, lifeless and dead as a spent rocket, he looked upon as demoralizing and dangerous. In writing to a friend on the subject, he once said that he had often noticed that "Christ never suffered sentimentalisms to pass without a matter-of-fact testing of what they were worth, and what they meant." And in his own life Robertson presented the

unusual spectacle of a man who combined
with the rapt exaltation and dreamy absent-
mindedness of the poet, the sternest fulfilment of every practical duty. All readers
of his biography know how unsparing —
culpably unsparing—he was of himself in
his ministerial work. In his sermons and
letters he again and again points out the
worthlessness of feeling, as opposed to
action. " Your lofty, incommunicable
thoughts," he says, " your ecstasies, and
aspirations, and contemplative raptures —
in virtue of which you have estimated
yourself as the porcelain of the earth,
of another nature altogether than the clay
of common spirits—tried by the test of
Charity what is there grand in these if they
cannot be applied as blessings to those that

are beneath you ?" And in another passage he tells us that, "To teach a few Sunday-School children, week after week, commonplace simple truths,—persevering in spite of dulness and mean capacities—is a more glorious occupation than the highest meditations or creations of genius which edify or instruct only our own solitary soul."

Hence so far from setting store by his reputation as a pulpiteer, his dislike to publicity was very marked. "Every mental nerve, so to speak," writes Mr. Brooke, "quivered with pain at being made the common talk and the wonder of a fashionable watering-place. If he hated one thing more than another, it was the reputation of being a popular preacher. He abhorred the very name as something which brought with it

I

contamination. A chivalrous gentleman, he shrank from the parade and show, the vulgarizing of his name, the obtrusion of his merits upon the public."

It is for this reason, perhaps, that Robertson's sermons are read, as the late Reverend Frederick Arnold has said, "by those who would refuse to read any other sermons. They have made and created sympathies in a class of minds into which the ordinary pulpiteer has no means of gaining admission."

And, indeed, it may be questioned whether there is any educated class whose testimony carries less weight with the outside world to-day, than that which follows religion as a profession. People are prone in these sceptical times to hold cheaply whatever is put forward in the pulpit. "Religion," they say, "is this man's trade, and it were strange indeed did he not cry up his own wares." But about Robertson there was nothing of the priest,—hardly even of the clergyman. In the pulpit, and out of it, he spoke neither as preacher to people, nor as teacher to pupil, but as man to man. He gave himself up to the service of others—not from a doleful sense of duty or of studied self-immolation, which he called God and men to witness, but because the human heart within him went out in love and sympathy to every human heart. And for sympathy Robertson had the strangest and rarest capability, though at what cost that gift of sympathy was attained, those who knew him best, best realized. "If you examine into it," says the Rev.

John Pulsford, "you will find that just in proportion as one is fitted to comfort, is his own liability to overwhelming distress. To be a real comforter, a person must have profound sympathies; but profound sympathies are always in association with keen sensibilities, and keen sensibilities expose their possessor to a depth of anguish utterly unintelligible to ordinary souls. As is the capacity to be a heavenly comforter, so is the capacity to be an awful sufferer."

Men knew, too, of Robertson that he preached no hearsay religion; but they knew equally well that he was no courter of doubts, no parader of the strange soul-questionings which assailed him, because he thought that such questionings marked him out as a profound or original thinker.

For years he accepted unhesitatingly the tenets of the Church of England ; but when his doubts came—as come they did with a suddenness and sternness which his biographer tells us "not only shook his health to its centre, but smote his spirit down into so profound a darkness, that of all his early faiths but one remained, 'it must be right to do right'"—he resolved that for him thenceforth there should be no building upon the sand. Fairly and squarely he looked his doubtings in the face, prepared, if need were, to relinquish his office in the ministry, prepared to part company with all that he valued on earth, rather than be false to conviction and to conscience. With the thoroughness which was so characteristic of the man he "took his entire theological system to pieces," as the Rev. Frederick Arnold has said, "and set to work to construct it anew." He would thenceforth accept no truth on hearsay. Each question, or aspect of a question, he approached as if it never had been approached before, and he seems even to have gone out of his way to seek evidence in support of his doubt, that he might know all that was to be said, and in facing it, face it once and for ever. Earnestness always and ever tells. It is contagious and it is convincing; and an earnest man with a bad case can gain more converts than one with less earnestness and a better cause.

III.

OF the noble work which, by means of this earnestness and his magnetic personality, Robertson did at Brighton, and of the immense influence for good he has since exerted on the world, this is not the place to speak. But in a paper which seeks to study certain aspects of the great preacher's personality, some mention must be made of the strange self-consciousness—the curse of many super-sensitive natures—which was so marked a feature in Robertson's individuality. In nearly all in whom the inward life is intense, and the outward life correspondingly subordinated, this self-consciousness is, in some degree, to be found; but in Robertson's case it was little less than a disease. It was, as it were, a second self from which he vainly strove to escape. He flung it from him and fled, thinking in the change and bustle of foreign travel to forget it, but it preceded him on his journey, and lay in ambush for him amid the cliffs of the Tyrol. It sat by his pillow as he sank to sleep, haunting even his dreams, and it kept unwinking watch by his bedside and was waiting to greet him when first his eyes were opened. Only in his work, and then not altogether, could he evade it, and although he aimed at keeping his sermons free from all obviously personal influences, yet in many of them this same self-consciousness is to be detected. It was partly due, as has been said, to the intensity of his inward life, and partly to the incommunicable soul-loneliness in which he lived. Such men as he are in the world, but not of it. They crave for the perfect sympathy which it is in the power of no human soul to give ; and, in the absence of which, they not seldom shrink back into shuddering and lonely self-consciousness which the world mistakes, not unnaturally, for pride.

The closing years of Robertson's life were darkened by terrible physical suffering, borne always with the gentle patience which was so characteristic of the man. " Torturing pain in the back of the head and neck, as if an eagle were rending there with his talons, made life dreadful to him," his biographer tells us. " Alone in his

room he lay on the rug, his head resting
on the bar of a chair, clenching his teeth
to prevent the groans which, even through
the sleepless length of solitary nights, the
ravaging pain could never draw from his
manliness. It is miserable to read, week
by week, the record of advancing illness,
and to know that it might have been
arrested by the repose which he did not,
and could not take."

He preached for the last time on Sunday,
June 5, 1853. Then followed three weeks'
terrible suffering, to which pitiful witness
is borne by the letters received from him
during this period. The handwriting, once
so firm and clear, looked, Mr. Brooke
tells us, as if it had been written "by one
just delivered from the rack. Every stroke

of the pen zigzags with the feebleness of pain." And yet in a letter which Robertson wrote shortly before his death to a friend, he said :—"God has treated me very mercifully. That I have felt in the direst pain and deepest exhaustion—the house filled with delicacies, presents . . . How different from the lot of Him who would fain 'have slaked his morning hunger on green figs'!" The last words he ever penned were to the same friend. "I shall never get over this," he said. "His will be done. I write in torture."

On Sunday, August 15, 1853, shortly after midnight, the end came. For two hours before his death he lay in the most awful anguish, feebly moaning, "My God, my Father! My God, my Father!" At last, in the hope of affording him some relief, his nurses proposed to change his position, but this he was unable to bear. "Let me rest. I must die. Let God do His work," he said; and then, without further word or sign, the spirit of Frederick Robertson passed away, and the life which this dreamer of dreams spoke of, and truly, as "a failure," was at an end.

A failure? Yes; for he aimed at perfect Christ-likeness in act and thought, and failed—not greatly. But as we think of the deep and perfect rest into which he has entered, the words of another "dreamer," and one whom Robertson loved — Jean Paul—rise to our thoughts: " There will come a time, when it shall be light ; and when man shall awaken from his lofty dreams, and find *his dreams still there, and that nothing has gone save his sleep.*"

PHILIP MARSTON, THE BLIND POET.

PHILIP BOURKE MARSTON.

DIED, FEB. 14, 1887.

GOD's angel, Sorrow, laid her hand on thee,
  And drew a deepening shroud across thine eyes,
  Shut out the windy sunsets' glimmering skies,
The shining stretches of the wide waste sea.
Then, with slow step, came One who sate, that she
  Might hold thine hand, with wan wet face and sighs
  Innumerable. "Men call me Grief," she cries;
"I live, and sleep, and eat and drink with thee."

Thus desolate days wore on till one drear night,
  Another step came nearer. "O long tried!"
Sudden a voice rang clear, "receive thy sight!"
  And at a touch thy dim eyes opened wide
To a great Darkness—and, in a great Light,
  Lost faces shining on the farther side.

MARY KERNAHAN.

PHILIP MARSTON, THE BLIND POET.

I.

ONE night in the 'seventies, when the late Dante Gabriel Rossetti, and the small and intimate group whose high privilege it was to enjoy his friendship and hospitality, were discussing poets and poetry, some one spoke of the difficulty of expressing a sense of infinite space in a few lines, and Philip Marston quoted, as a successful example, the sestette of Rossetti's sonnet, " The Choice " :—

"Nay, come up hither. From this wave-washed mound
  Unto the furthest flood-brim look with me ;
Then reach on with thy thought till it be drown'd.
  Miles and miles distant though the last line be,
And though thy soul sail leagues and leagues beyond,—
  Still, leagues beyond those leagues, there is more sea."

The next day, Rossetti was looking over Marston's *Songtide*, and said to him, "You spoke last night about the sestette of 'The Choice' being fine, Philip, but this line of yours is worth all my six," and he pointed out in the blind poet's sonnet, "Wedded Grief," the line,

"Whose sea conjectures of no further land."

On another occasion, when Marston was not present, the name of Arthur O'Shaughnessy was mentioned, and the excellence of his lyrics commended.

"Yes," said Rossetti, "O'Shaughnessy

has done some good work, but that Philip Marston stands at the head of all the younger men is, I think, beyond question."

This was high praise from such a quarter, but Rossetti's estimate of Marston will always, to some extent, be discounted by those who remember that the blind poet was himself of the school of which the poet-painter was the acknowledged master.

And indeed it was an unfortunate, as well as a fortunate thing for Marston, that when Fate set him to sing darkling (as men veil a songbird's cage that it may more readily learn each note), the voice from the outer world which he was ever quick to distinguish, was the voice of Dante Rossetti. Fortunate, for the reason that Marston could

scarcely have chosen a more consummate
master of song under whom to perfect the
gift with which himself was endowed; unfortunate, because the blind poet's ardent
love and reverence for his master led him
so to saturate himself with his master's
work, that his thoughts took colouring from
Rossetti to an extent which tended to subor-
dinate his own individuality.   Hence there
are passages in the poems of the younger
singer which inevitably recall similar passages in those of the elder, and a comparison
is thus instituted which it is no serious dis-
paragement of Marston to say is not to his
advantage.   In lyric loveliness and grace
some of the blind poet's work is not unworthy of comparison with Rossetti's, but
we miss in Marston's lines the deep-mouthed

volume of sound, the rhythmic splendour
and sonority which are rarely absent from
the poet-painter's. For all its sweetness,
Marston's voice seems thin and shrill after
Rossetti's, and the framework of his poetry
strikes one as lacking in intellectual robust-
ness. He is diffuse, and often painfully un-
equal; for, although his poems are never
wanting in grace and fluency, he had that
fatal facility for verse-making which often
leads to the publication of much that is
mediocre and immature. Melody is his one
unfailing characteristic, and musical his lines
always are. The harp he touched was
strung with silvern chords attuned to subtle
sweetness, but his range of music was
narrow, and his bass notes were few. There
were times when, under the influence of a

stirring thought, he beat out a strain of solemn grandeur, but most of his melodies are set to a minor key, and are rendered more or less monotonous by an ever-recurrent note of sadness. His poetry has been called "gloomy," and gloomy indeed much of it is; but as one sometimes hears, ringing from a darkened chamber of mourning, cries which condense a whole life-history into half-a-dozen passionate words—so from the perpetual darkness in which the blind poet lived, there arose a voice athrill with such intensity of feeling, that men, hearing it, paused involuntarily to listen. Here is a sonnet addressed by Marston to his dead love, in which the lines seem shaken with suppressed sobs.

"It must have been for one of us, my own,
  To drink this cup, and eat this bitter bread.
  Had not my tears upon thy face been shed,
Thy tears had dropped on mine; if I alone
Did not walk now, thy spirit would have known
  My loneliness; and did my feet not tread
  This weary path and steep, thy feet had bled
For mine, and thy mouth had for mine made moan.

And so it comforts me, yea, not in vain,
  To think of thine eternity of sleep;
  To know thine eyes are tearless though mine weep;
And when this cup's last bitterness I drain,
  One thought shall still its primal sweetness keep—
Thou hadst the peace, and I the undying pain."

II.

THERE is no truer test whereby to distinguish the poet "born" from the poet "made" than the writing of a lyric; and if the name of Philip Marston is to live in English literature, it will be by his flower-

lyrics, or *Garden Secrets* as he called them,
and the best of his sonnets. A flower,
especially a sweet-scented one, never failed
to move him deeply. Time had robbed
him of love, and hope, and the most
cherished of his friendships, and there had
gathered around him a mental gloom,
blacker even than the physical darkness
in which he lived, as in a house of which
he was the only tenant—a darkness which
seemed to him, at the last, like a charnel
chamber strewn with the ashes of dead
hope, dead love, and dead aspiration. But
a flower, fair, fresh, and immortal, as in the
days of his youth, and to him the one
unchanging and perfect thing in a changing
and decaying world, would call forth new
hope within him, and would waken in the

heart of the blinded, sorrow-stricken poet, some memory of his happier self. Hence he could scarcely speak of flowers without his words rising into poetry, and he has personified them in language which recalls the ripple and run, the lightness and lilt, of the Elizabethans.

All this is done with true simplicity. We never find ourselves wondering at the quaintness of the idea, for it seems as natural that roses should whisper and laugh among themselves in Marston's verses, as that birds should sing and waters flow. It is not the blind poet who is telling us *his* fancies: it is the flowers themselves to which we are listening, and all he has done is to let us into the secret of their language. He takes us into a world of fairyland, in which we forget the worries and the weariness of the workaday world we have left behind.

Rossetti, who, notwithstanding his severity as a critic, sometimes let his characteristic generosity towards the men with whom he was most in sympathy betray him into extravagance, once said of these *Garden Secrets* that they were " worthy of Shakespeare in his subtlest lyrical moods." Not many will feel free to follow the poet-painter in this excess of enthusiasm ; but that Mr. Theodore Watts was justified in saying of " The Rose and the Wind," which I quote below, that "so perfect a lyric ought to entitle Marston to an independent place of his own, and that no inconsiderable one," few will dispute.

THE ROSE AND THE WIND.

DAWN.

The Rose.

WHEN think you comes the Wind,
The Wind that kisses me and is so kind?
Lo, how the Lily sleeps! her sleep is light;
Would I were like the Lily, pale and white!
Will the Wind come?

The Beech.

Perchance for thee too soon.

The Rose.

If not, how could I live until the noon?
What, think you, Beech-tree, makes the Wind delay?
Why comes he not at breaking of the day?

The Beech.

Hush, child, and, like the Lily, go to sleep.

The Rose.

You know I cannot.

The Beech.

Nay, then, do not weep.
(*After a pause.*)
Thy lover comes, be happy now, O Rose!
He softly through my bending branches goes.
Soon he shall come, and you shall feel his kiss.

The Rose.

Already my flushed heart grows faint with bliss;
Love, I have longed for thee through all the night.

The Wind.

And I to kiss thy petals warm and bright.

The Rose.

Laugh round me, Love, and kiss me; it is well.
Nay, have no fear; the Lily will not tell.

MORNING.

The Rose.

'Twas dawn when first you came; and now the sun
Shines brightly, and the dews of dawn are done.
'Tis well you take me so in your embrace,
But lay me back again into my place,
For I am worn, perhaps with bliss extreme.

The Wind.

Nay, you must wake, Love, from this childish dream.

The Rose.

'Tis thou, Love, seemest changed; thy laugh is loud,
And 'neath thy stormy kiss my head is bowed.
O Love, O Wind, a space wilt thou not spare?

The Wind.

Not while thy petals are so soft and fair!

The Rose.

My buds are blind with leaves, they cannot see.
O Love, O Wind, wilt thou not pity me?

EVENING.

The Beech.

O Wind! a word with you before you pass :
What did you to the Rose, that on the grass
Broken she lies, and pale, who loved you so?

The Wind.

Roses must live and love, and winds must blow.

Scent and sound, to both of which he
was singularly susceptible, Marston has
interwoven into his work with rare skill.
Some of his lyrics have the trickle and purl
of running water, and the pages of his
Garden Secrets seem pervaded with the
delicate perfume of the lily and rose. Nor
are effects of light and shade, of colour
and tone—the last things to be expected
in the poems of a blind man—rare in
his verses. Who would suspect that the

writer of the following lines, for instance,
was sightless ?

"Now when the time of the sun's setting came,
                    The sky caught flame;
  For all the sun, which as an empty name
  Had been that day, then rent the leaden veil,
  And flashed out sharp, 'twixt watery clouds, and pale :
  Then suddenly a stormy wind upsprang,
                    That shrieked and sang;
  Around the reeling tree-tops, loud it rang,
  And all was dappled blue, and faint, fresh gold,
  Lovely and virgin ; wild, and sweet, and cold."

Of the wind, as well as of flowers,
Marston has written with singular power
and beauty :—

"Blow, autumn wind of this tempestuous night!
    Roar through this garden, and bear down these trees;
    Surely to-night thy voice is as the seas,
  And all my heart exultant in thy might."

With the wind, indeed, he had always
a strange sympathy ; and one is tempted,

at times, to fancy that it was to the accompaniment, and under the inspiration of Æolian music that certain of his poems were written; for in the wind harp's fitful strain—now sighing in and out among the strings, soft and low, and scarcely audible; now upswelling to a shrill and stormy cry of passionate sorrow, but always sweet, and most musically mournful—there is that which strangely recalls the voice of the blind poet, and which seems to suggest the source and secret of his singing.

III.

MARSTON died on February 14, 1887; and in 1891 his unpublished poems were collected and issued under the title of *A*

Last Harvest. Peculiar interest and significance are lent to this volume by the fact that it made its appearance after his death. There is always something of mystery and pathos in the birth of a posthumous child. The reminder which such an event gives us of the certainty with which our acts work on to inevitable results, even though we are not here to witness these results, is singularly impressive. It is, too, a strange reversal of the order of things to reflect that the little fluttering spark of life, which any ungentle wind might puff out—the very type and symbol of all that is feeble and dependent,— is less helpless than the strong man from whom it took its being, but who lies in leaden inactivity, and incapable of as much as a finger-stir.

And what is true of the children of the body, is, to an extent, true of the children of the brain ; for just as we search the face of a posthumous child for some resemblance to the features of the parent who will never be seen on earth again, so do we scan the pages of *A Last Harvest*—the posthumous child of Philip Marston's brain— for that which recalls the singer who has gone out from us.

The first question which will be asked is, whether the volume is an advance upon Marston's previous work, and to that question the answer is both "yes" and "no." Yes, in the sense that a higher artistic level of workmanship is maintained throughout; no, inasmuch as it contains, with one exception, no sonnet or lyric which

L

is distinctively finer of its sort than anything to be found in his previous work. The most notable poem in the collection is the opening lyric, in which, under the metaphor of " Love's Pleasure-House," Marston sings his worship of the physical beauty of womanhood. In the haunting witchery of its melody, the poem recalls Edgar Allan Poe at his best.

"Love built for himself a Pleasure-House,—
    A Pleasure-House fair to see:
The roof was gold, and the walls thereof
    Were delicate ivory.

Violet crystal the windows were,
    All gleaming and fair to see;
Pillars of rose-stained marble up-bore
    That house where men longed to be.

Violet, golden, and white and rose,
    That Pleasure-House fair to see
Did show to all; and they gave Love thanks
    For work of such mastery.

Love turned away from his Pleasure-House,
  And stood by the salt, deep sea :
He looked therein, and he flung therein
  Of his treasure the only key.

Now never a man till time be done
  That Pleasure-House fair to see
Shall fill with music and merriment,
  Or praise it on bended knee."

It was a happy thought of Mrs. Moulton's (the editor of the volume) to set this fine lyric in the entrance-hall of Philip Marston's last House of Poetry. It stands there, like an alabaster Venus awakening to warm life, in the portico of a temple of the Muses. And in regard to Mrs. Moulton it should be observed, in this connection, that the story of her loving ministration to the blind poet when he was living, and of her devotion to his memory when he was dead, will, when it comes to be told, form one of the most beautiful and touching chapters in the history of literary friendships. "Ah! I shall soon be under the daisies," Marston said to me once in a despondent mood. " I suppose there will be a short obituary in the *Athenæum* and the *Academy*, and a line or two in the daily and weekly papers, but before a year is out, I and my work will be forgotten." That the grace and beauty of some of his lyrics and sonnets would amply and alone suffice to keep his memory green, must be apparent to every student of English poetry ; but it is nevertheless a fact that but for the loving and unselfish labours of Mrs. Moulton and of Marston's brother-singer and loyal friend, Mr. William Sharp, his work would be far less widely known and appreciated than it is.

The most remarkable feature in *A Last Harvest* is the high average excellence of the sonnets.   Here is one which, if somewhat conventional in conception, is finely expressed :—

TO-MORROW.

"I said 'To-morrow!' one bleak, winter day—
   'To-morrow I will live my life anew,'—
   And still 'To-morrow!' while the winter grew
To spring, and yet I dallied by the way,
And sweet, dear Sins still held me in their sway.
   'To-morrow!' I said, while summer days wore
      through ;
   'To-morrow!' while chill autumn round me drew ;
And so my soul remained the sweet Sins' prey.

So pass the years, and still, perpetually,
   I cry, 'To-morrow will I flee each wile ;—
To-morrow, surely, shall my soul stand free,
   Safe from the siren voices that beguile !'
   But Death waits by me, with a mocking smile,
And whispers—'Yea! To-morrow, verily !'"

The defect in this sonnet is, of course, the rhyming of "verily" and "perpetually" in

the sestette.   Where the constant repetition
of perfect rhymes tends, in a degree, to
become monotonous, and to weary the
ear, a skilful variation enhances rather than
lessens the beauty of a poem.   This
must be done, it need scarcely be said,
with a very dexterous hand, for any care-
less rhyming in so delicate a piece of
workmanship as a sonnet, not only breaks
the measured "marking time" (like the
marching of a multitude), which is the
result of the recurrence of the rhyme at
regular intervals, but is a distinct defect.
Strangely enough—for an unerring ear is
the one thing we might have expected in a
blind man—Marston is occasionally at fault
in this respect, not only in his earlier
work, but in his latest volume.   For just

as in *Wind-Voices* he used "hear" and "here" as rhymes, so he uses "blew" and "blue" in the following exquisite sonnet from *A Last Harvest* :—

"The breadth and beauty of the spacious night
    Brimmed with white moonlight, swept by winds that blew
    The flying sea-spray up to where we two
Sat all alone, made one in Love's delight,—
The sanctity of sunsets, palely bright;
    Autumnal woods, seen 'neath meek skies of blue;
    Old cities that God's silent peace stole through,—
These of our love were very sound and sight.

The strain of labour; the bewildering din
    Of thundering wheels; the bells' discordant chime;
    The sacredness of art; the spell of rhyme,—
These, too, with our dear love were woven in,
    That so, when parted, all things might recall
    The sacred love that had its part in all."

The use of the rhymed couplet with which Marston, as in this instance, so frequently concludes his sonnets, is of course strictly legitimate, and indeed is often desirable for the sake of variety and convenience. But in sonnets not formed upon the Shakespearian model, the more delicate and distant decline of the rhyme (like the indistinguishable dying away of sweet music) is, I think, more harmonious.

IV.

Not the least remarkable characteristic of Marston's mournful and musical verses is his constant anticipation of death. Even at the very outset of his journey, and as he was groping his way in his sunless, starless solitude, Philip Marston found that all life's sign-posts pointed for him in one of two directions—"To Love," or "To Death"; nor was it long before, following the path to Love, he found it lead to, and lose itself in the path to Death ; and from thenceforth and for ever the thought of Death was never long absent from his mind.

Here is a mournful fancy, in which, speaking of the time when he and those whom he loves shall—

"Lie at the last beneath where the grass grows, .
    Made one in one interminable repose,
Not knowing whence we came or whither went "—

he asks himself if there will not linger in the room, "the desolate, ghost-thronged room" where he had lived, and loved, and suffered, some haunting memory of him who was so long its tenant :—

"Must this not be, that one then dwelling here,
　　Where one man and his sorrows dwelt so long,
　　Shall feel the pressure of a ghostly throng,
And shall upon some desolate midnight hear
　　A sound more sad than is the pine-trees' song,
And thrill with great, inexplicable fear?"

And in *A Last Harvest* there is a poem entitled "Alas!" written in Marston's later years, when ill-health and misfortune had had their cruel will of him, which, hopeless and pessimistic though it may be, yet voices the inarticulate cry of many a human heart.

"Alas for all high hopes and all desires !
　　Like leaves in yellow autumn-time they fall ;
Alas for prayers and psalms and love's pure fires—
　　One silence and one darkness ends them all !

Alas for all the world—sad fleeting race !
　　Alas, my Love, for you and me, Alas !
Grim Death will clasp us in his close embrace,
　　We, too, like all the rest from earth must pass.

Alas to think we must forget some hours
  Whereof the memory like Love's planet glows—
Forget them as the year her withered flowers—
  Forget them as the June forgets the rose!

Our keenest rapture, our most deep despair,
  Our hopes, our dreads, our laughter, and our tears,
Shall be no more at all upon the air—
  No more at all, through all the endless years.

We shall be mute beneath the grass and dew
  In that dark Kingdom where Death reigns in
    state—
And you will be as I, and I as you—
  One silence shed upon us and one fate."

It seems to me that these lines of Marston's must have a strange pathos to all who read them when the grass grows thick on his grave, and who have still to learn the right answer to that questioning cry which rose so often to his lips: "Ah! if only I knew what lay beyond!" But to some of us who remember the gentle-hearted poet, the lovable and unselfish friend, death seems less like an iron curtain, let down between us and our lost ones, than like the blinds we set in our windows, —blinds which from the outside look black and impenetrable, but which from the inside scarce serve to soften the light. And, at times, we seem to see—close-pressed against the window of the House of Death into which he has passed—the face of Philip Marston loom out into the night; and in the sightless eyes (sightless never again) we see a look of tender and infinite pity for us who have yet to face the mystery which he has solved.

THE END.

WARD, LOCK, AND BOWDEN, LTD., LONDON, NEW YORK, AND MELBOURNE.

www.ingramcontent.com/pod-product-compliance
Lightning Source LLC
Chambersburg PA
CBHW020015030726
47500CB00002B/597